Harry Warren Yearick

Memoirs of Harry Warren Yearick and his ancestors for five generations

Harry Warren Yearick

Memoirs of Harry Warren Yearick and his ancestors for five generations

ISBN/EAN: 9783337124359

Printed in Europe, USA, Canada, Australia, Japan

Cover: Foto ©Raphael Reischuk / pixelio.de

More available books at **www.hansebooks.com**

Memoirs of

HARRY WARREN YEARICK

and

HIS ANCESTORS _

for

FIVE GENERATIONS

#

1899

PREFACE

Believing, in common with many others, the importance of the
scriptural passage: "Honor thy father and thy mother: that thy
days may be long upon the land which the Lord thy God giveth thee."
(Ex. XX-12), the author has prepared these memoirs. The scriptural
passage is a command direct from God, and if lived up to in youth
will prove a blessing in old age.

The honor in which a parent is held, should live in the memory of
the children and their children for many generations. This was
impressed upon the author by his father, who left him much valuable
information regarding his ancestors before his spirit was recalled
to its Maker. To the mother of the author is due his highest appre-
ciation for her valuable assistance in perfecting these memoirs,
which, had she not been possessed of a wonderful memory, would have
been very incomplete.

These memoirs have been prepared that later generations may know
of their ancestors and do honor to their memory. To the author's
children, should he be so blessed, these memoirs are lovingly
dedicated by

H. W. Yearick

INDEX OF NAMES

Part I

HARRY WARREN YEARICK

Harry Warren Yearick was born on Monday, the 15th day of April, in the year 1878, at Toledo, Ohio. His first home was situated on the west side of Fifteenth street, between Washington and Monroe streets. He was educated in the public and grammar schools of the city, and at the age of sixteen years entered the employ of Foncannon & Co., druggists, in the capacity of house-to-house advertiser. On October 15, 1894, he took a position with that firm as clerk in their store, 101 Summit St.

Mr. Yearick left the employ of Foncannon & Co., January 30, 1897, and shortly entered the newspaper field, which afterwards became his chosen profession. Right here it is fitting to state that while attending school he earned his own spending money by working up a newspaper route, delivering papers to his customers for a number of years.

He first obtained employment in the newspaper field on the Toledo Evening News, as reporter under A. Riley Crittenden, then city editor, and commenced work February 25, 1897. His first assignment was the opening of a new dry goods house by Leahy, Kilduff & Purcell at 405 Summit St. On the News he advanced from a green to an experienced reporter and up to the time of writing had, at different times covered all of the regular beats. When these memoirs were written he was looking after police, sport and markets, to which he had become very attached, excepting markets.

DELINEATION OF CHARACTER

A delineation of the character, physiological development and condition at that time of Mr. Yearick was given by H. E. Swain, physiologist, about 1882, and is as follows: Organic quality, large; health, average; vital temperment, average; breathing power, full; circulatory power, full; digestive power, average; motive temperment, between full and average; mental temperment, large; activity, between large and full; excitability, full; size of brain, large; amativeness (love between the sexes, desire to marry, full: conjugality, full; parental love, large; friendship, large; inhabitiveness (love of home and country), between large and full; continuity, between full and large, acquisitiveness, average; cautiousness, large; self respect, average; firmness, full; spirituality, full; veneration, large; benevolence, between very large and large; constructiveness, full; ideality, large; mirthfulness, between full and average; individuality, large; perception and love of method, system, etc., full; cognizance of numbers, mental arithmetic, between large and full; locality (recollection of places and scenery), between large and full: memory of facts and circumstances, very large; time (cognizance of duration and succession of time, punctuality), full; language (expression of ideas, memory of words), large; causality (applying causes to effect, originaltiy) between very large and large; humane nature (perception of character and motives) average; agreeableness (pleasantness, suavity, persuasiveness) between large and full.

I

The parents of Mr. Yearick were Joseph Peter Yearick and Adelaide
Yearick, nee Warren. They had three children, Harry Warren, Anna
Mabel, and Joseph Arthur. Mabel was born September 27, 1879 and
married Edward P. McGrath of Toledo, November 29, 1899. (They are
the parents of two children, Dorothy Adelaide, born June 20, 1901,
and Edward Arnold McGrath, born Sept. 25, 1902.

Joseph A. Yearick was born August 3, 1881. He married Josie Nichter
of Toledo, Ohio, December 12, 1907. They have two daughters, Adelaide
and Jeannette.

Harry Warren Yearick was married to Edna Freeman of Toledo, Ohio, on
the 18th day of April 18, 1901 by Rev. F. P. Rosselot. Mrs. Yearick
was born February 1, 1883, at Toledo, to Eli R. Freeman and Erexina
Freeman, nee Roberts. A sister, Bessie, died in infancy. A brother,
Homer, was born February 25, 1891. (He died about 1964 in Florida,
leaving a widow, Emma, and four children, Howard, Kenneth, Dorothy,
and Virginia, now Mrs. James Bratcher, 2612 52nd Avenue N., St.
Petersburg, Florida.)

Mr. and Mrs. H. W. Yearick are the parents of the following children:

Warren Freeman	b. 1901	d. 1946	
Stanley Roberts	b. 1903	married	Irene Riley
Roland Milton	b. 1905	"	Caroline Krienbihl
Edna Mabelle	b. 1908	"	Harold Reifsnider
Marian Thirza	b. 1912	"	Winton O. Etz
Harry Gordon	b. 1916	"	Willie Mae Williamson
Carroll Homer	b. 1919	"	Clara Rebecca Campbell
Margery Adelia	b. 1924	"	Earl H. Pepiot
Donald Walter	b. 1927	"	Lorraine Vance

II

JOSEPH PETER YEARICK

Joseph Peter Yearick was born in Ashland County, Ohio, June 3, 1843, and died at his home, 851 Colfax Street, Toledo, Ohio, Sunday, July 19, 1896, at the age of 53 years, 1 month and 16 days. Between those dates he filled in a life of quiet unostentatious usefulness. His boyhood days were mostly spent in Iowa. When his country called for men during the Civil war, he responded, but because of nearsightedness, was rejected. His was one of those natures which never allowed any obstacle to keep him from performing what he thought to be his duty. When, therefore, he could not go to the front, he secured a position as teamster of a wagon train and was stationed at Nashville. Later he was transferred to Chattanooga, where he served until the war closed.

In 1875 he came to Toledo to work at his trade, carpentering, and met Miss Adelaide Warren, to marry whom he returned the following year, and lived there the rest of his life. The Toledo Evening News of July 20, 1896, had the following to say regarding Mr. Yearick.

> "His health has gradually grown worse for months past with a heart trouble. Seven weeks ago he gave up, and yesterday noon the end came. In the neighborhood of his home Mr. Yearick is mourned by everyone. His nature was one of those which developed into a warm true friendship for all he knew, and his sterling Christian qualities elevated everyone with whom he came in contact. He was a member of Toledo lodge, F. and A. M. and Carpenters' Union."

Funeral services for Mr. Yearick were held from the family residence Tuesday afternoon, and the remains interred in the beautiful Woodlawn cemetery at Toledo. The family burial lot at Woodlawn is the undivided one half of the Northwest 1/2 of lot #197, section 27.

Mr. Yearick invented a roller coaster about 1884, known as Yearick's Gravity Railway. (U. S. Patent granted April 28, 1885, No. 316512. Canada Patent granted August 1885.) This railway was designed as a means of amusement in which the cars were impelled by gravity and velocity. Before Mr. Yearick's invention such railways had been continuous and circular, or nearly so, and by reason of such shape, necessarily occupied considerable space, an objectional feature in cities, where such railways were operated. Mr. Yearick's patent obviated the objection and was so arranged that the cars traveled to and fro alternately in opposit directions, their motion being reversed automatically by gravitation.

When Mr. Yearick disposed of his patent he invested the proceeds of the sale in forty-seven shares of the Smith & Haldeman Elevator Co. capital stock for his wife. This investment was made on February 9, 1888, and proved a rank failure in time.

The following is a true copy of a document which Mr. Yearick prepared showing his war record.

Toledo, Ohio, May 7, 1895

In March 1864 I was employed by a government agent at Iowa City as a post teamster and was sent to Nashville, Tenn., and after two or three days was transferred to Chattanooga, Tenn. General Thomas was post commander. I served there eleven months with a man by the name of Wm. Murdock, of an Illinois regiment as wagon or train master. I do not remember the number of his regiment. I was known by the boys as the Iowa boy, but discharged in February 1865 in my real name. I was not mustered in or out in the ordinary way, simply employed and when I got ready to go home given my time of service, an order to draw my pay and half transportation home.

- Joseph P. Yearick.

The parents of Mr. Yearick were Peter Yearick and Anna Catherine Yearick, nee Gutelius.

Mrs. Adelaide Yearick, nee Warren, was born February 21, 1841, in
Orleans County, New York, town of Jeddo on the ridge road from Buffalo
to Rochester. This ridge road, although ten miles from Lake Ontario,
is supposed to have at one time been the shore of the lake.

When Mrs. Yearick was about three years old, her father, William
Perkins Warren, moved west with his family. They came overland with
only a team and wagon to transport their household goods, and settled
out of Toledo on the Bancroft road at Five Points. After they had
been there but a short time the whole family was taken down with the
fever and ague, which were prevalant around Toledo for many years. It
took the Warrens some time to become aclimated.

Two years were spent at Five Points, during which time Mr. Warren
cleared enough land near Sulphur Springs to build a log house. Here
he brought his family. This rude habitation had no doors or windows
the first winter, and blankets had to be put up to the openings to
keep out the cold. The nearest road to this place, which the Warrens
called home, was at Five Points, and to get there a stream had to be
forded. A railroad, however, ran through the farm. This road had
its terminal at Adrian, Michigan.

When Mrs. Yearick was eleven years old her mother died, and even though
a little girl, she kept house for the children for two months. During
this time her father was doing carpenter work in Toledo and only came
home on Saturday nights, staying over Sunday. Mr. Warren was a smoker,
but became disgusted with the habit while working in Toledo, gave it
up and never smoked thereafter. What disgusted him was the sight of
young boys in the city with either pipe or cigar in their mouths.

3

At the end of the two months, during which time Mrs. Yearick kept house
for the children, her father became convinced that it was not safe to
leave them alone. Then for about two months the children boarded out,
but were not treated well. The father learned of this and shortly went
back east with his children to York state, where they remained until he
married a second time, coming back to their Ohio home to live.

When Mrs. Yearick was seventeen years old she again went back to York
state, this time alone, and remained there about a year. Then she came
back to stay and taught school at Palmyra, Michigan, for one winter.
The people at Palmyra wanted her to come back the next summer, but she
decided not to and thereafter worked in the city (Toledo), doing dress
making, millinary, and clerking until the time of her marriage to
Joseph Peter Yearick.

Mr. and Mrs. Yearick were married December 27, 1876, at the First Congre-
gational church of Toledo, by the Reverend W. W. Williams.

Mrs. Yearick's parents were William Perkins Warren and Sarah Warren,
nee Bull.

PART III

MR. AND MRS. PETER YEARICK

Mr. and Mrs. Peter Yearick were married May 10, 1818, by Rev. Henry
Friese at Mifflinburg, Pa. They moved to Ashland (then Wayne) county,
Ohio, in the spring of 1834, and then to Johnson County, Iowa, in the
spring of 1855. They returned to Ashland County in the fall of 1871,
and in May 1872, moved to Findlay, Ohio.

Peter Yearick was born on February 14, 1798, in Lohill township, North
Hampton County, Pa., and died Saturday, January 17, 1885, of Bright's
disease of the kidneys, at the home of his daughter, Mrs. Elvina Goodwin, in North Findlay, Ohio, at the age of eighty-seven years and 28
days. At the time of his death the following appeared in a Findlay
newspaper:

> "The death of Father Yearick ends a remarkably useful and
> exemplary life. Nearly a year ago, his faithful companion
> died after they had spent over sixty-six years in the matri-
> monial relation and had reared twelve children, all of whom
> are still living. Mr. Yearick had been a faithful and con-
> sistant Christian and a member of the Evangelical church
> for over sixty-five years. For nearly a year past his
> health has been feeble and he constantly hoped for the end.
> The funeral services occurred Monday afternoon, Rev. W. W.
> Sherrick officiating."

The family record of Peter Yearick's antecedants is very incomplete.
His father died at the age of thirty-two years, and the widow married
Andrew Gnorr. She died at the age of eighty-eight years. Peter and
Daniel Yearick are the only children of whom there is any record.
Daniel Yearick died in 1882 at the age of eight-two years.

(The following note was pencilled in the margin: Penna Dutch
P. Jarck/in letter file)

Mrs. Anna Catherine Yearick, nee Gutelius, the wife of Peter Yearick, was born July 25, 1800, at Monhime, Lancaster county, Pa., and died March 23, 1884, at Findlay, Ohio, after six years of great suffering. She was a worthy Christian, amiable mother, and died very happy. She left twelve children (two having gone before) and a husband to mourn her departure. At the time of her death, which was caused by gangrene, she was eight-three years, seven months and twenty-eight days old. The funeral was held on March 25 and was conducted by Elder Crouse, assisted by Rev. Shericks. The service consisted of the reading of Psalm XC; text: Rev. VII, 9 and 10; hymns: "Asleep in the Arms of Jesus" and "Why Should We Fear to Die?" Present at the funeral were: Children - Gutelius Israel, Joseph Peter, Anna Caroline, Elizabeth and Elvina; grand-children - Elnora Goodwin, and Joe Goodwin and family; niece - Mrs. Anna M. Lucas.

The parents of Mrs. Anna Catherine Yearick were Frederick Gutelius and Catherine Gutelius, nee Bistel.

To Mr. and Mrs. Peter Yearick were born the following children: Elvina, Sussanna, Henry Edward, Elizabeth, Gutelius Israel, Anna Caroline, Frederick Emanuel, Sarah Catherine, Rebecca Sussanna, Samuel William, Mary Ann, John Agustus, Joseph Peter and Simon Amandas.

ELVINA YEARICK
Elvina Yearick was born September 10, 1820, at Hoftinburg, Union County, Pa.; married to John Goodwin on February 13, 1840, and died on Monday July 3, 1893, at Findlay, Ohio, after a brief illness that gave no sign of its sad ending. The funeral services were held the following Thursday, and a large number of friends were present to testify to the love and esteem in which she was held in the community of which she was a prominent and honored member. Mrs. Goodwin was at one time a resident of Ashland, Ohio, and was remembered there for her many noble qualities.

6

John Goodwin, the husband of Elvina, died November 18, 1880. To Mr. and Mrs. John Goodwin were born Joe H. Goodwin on February 25, 1841. Samuel Goodwin was born February 11, 1845, and died August 11, 1851. Sarah Goodwin was born February 11, 1847, and died July 18, 1871. John William Goodwin was born May 6, 1849, and died the same day. Mrs. Mary Barnd, nee Goodwin, was born December 3, 1851, and died February 19, 1883. Gutelius Goodwin was born December 15, 1854, and died May 3, 1876. Mrs. Elnora Boyd, nee Goodwin, was born August 6, 1857. Charles Goodwin was born May 23, 1860.

SUSSANNA YEARICK

Sussanna Yearick was born October 27, 1821 at Mifflinburg, Union County, Pa., and died February 16, 1824.

HENRY EDWARD YEARICK

Henry Edward Yearick was born December 23, 1823, at Mifflinburg, Union County, Pa., and died Tuesday, September 5, 1893, at Washington, Iowa. He located in Johnson County, Iowa, in 1853 and moved to Washington, Iowa, in 1864. A third wife and two children, albert S., of Bushnell, Ill., and Mrs. Alice M. Armstrong, wife of Samuel M. Armstrong of Chicago, survived him. Mr. Yearick's health had been failing for a long time and he was confined to the house for three or four months before he died.

The funeral occurred the following Thursday, the religious service being conducted by Rev. B. E. S. Ely, Jr. After these exercises, the Masonic fraternity, deceased being a K. T., took charge of the remains and the interment was conducted by them. Dr. Yearick of Cedar Rapids, John Yearick and Ed Taylor of Iowa City, Mrs. Johnson and Mrs. Adams, relatives, of Sigourney, and Mr. Mintier of the same place, attended the funeral.

ELIZABETH YEARICK

Elizabeth Yearick was born December 11, 1825, at Brushvalley, Center County, Pa., and died Saturday evening, May 10, 1890, at her home in Ashland, Ohio, on Sandusky street. On Saturday morning she did all

her housework and was evidently in as good health as at any other time.
In the afternoon she repaired to the U. B. church with her horse and
buggy in order to be present at the baptism of several new members.
As this event had been postponed, she commenced her homeward journey.
Before reaching home a storm burst forth in vehemence. On reaching
home she was compelled to be carried from the buggy, and before a bed
was reached she expired. The physician in attendance was of the opin-
ion that death resulted from a paralytic stroke superinduced by fright.

On the 7th day of November, 1843, Elizabeth Yearick became Mrs. Shutt.
Her husband, John Shutt, was born September 18, 1821, and died Septem-
ber 25, 1876. He was an earnest Christian and member of the U. B.
Church for twenty-five years.

Mrs. Shutt married a second time on October 4, 1881, taking to husband
Peter Newcomer, who died January 24, 1899, at the ripe old age of
eighty years, ten months and thirteen days.

To Mr. and Mrs. Shutt were born five children. Henry Philip Shutt was
born July 23, 1844, and married Lizzie Powers on the 8th day of February, 1864. He served three years in the Union army, commencing 1861.
Mary Jane Shutt was born February 8, 1846; married William Pittenger
February 21, 1866. Sarah Catherine Shutt was born December 31, 1847;
married Daniel Wile October 1, 1866. Caroline Luella Shutt was born
February 23, 1850; died June 3, 1859. Willie Shutt was born September
3, 1851; died June 3, 1859.

GUTELIUS ISRAEL YEARICK

Gutelius Israel Yearick was born August 11, 1827, at Raversburg,
Center County, Pa., and died on August 3, 1898, at his home in Ashland,
Ohio. The following article from one of the Ashland newspapers gives
his complete biography.

Though Guelius I. Yearick, a prominent citizen of Ashland, had been in
ill health off and on for several years, yet his end came suddenly
and sharply after all. He died last Wenesday night about 10 o'clock
at his home on Claremont Avenue. He had just passed into one of the

rooms of the house when he was attacked with heart failure, and fell
to the floor. He was assisted to rise, and medical attendance was
hastily summoned, but he lived but a short time.

Mr. Yearick was peculiarly a leading citizen of Ashland. His habits
and manners were his own and he had the happy faculty of making
acquaintances easily. Owing to the nature of his business and to his
unusual social qualities he was well known not only over the county,
but in adjoining counties. He was sociable and friendly to everyone,
and in the prime of his life took great pleasure in society. He was
Chesterfieldian in his public deportment, and was graceful in social
functions. He took part in politics and became prominent in this way
also. He was genial, kindhearted and liberal in character, and al-
ways impressed those who became acquainted with hime by his striking
appearance.

According to the record in his own family Bible, he was born at
Mifflinburg, Pa., August 11, 1829, although the general impression
has been that he was more than sixty-nine years old. When a small
boy he removed with his parents to Redhaw, this county, and at the
age of twelve years he was apprenticed to a turner. He worked at his
trade in Ashland and in western Ohio and eastern Indiana until 1855,
when he returned to Ashland and engaged in the furniture business.
About 1856 he suffered a heavy loss by fire. He continued in the furniture business until 1860, when he sold out to Col. D. J. Stubbs.
In 1861, he enlisted in the 82nd O. V. I., and became a recruiting
officer. After the war, Mr. Yearick engaged in the loan agency business, and followed that until 1869, when he was elected county
treasurer on the Democratic ticket, he being greatly devoted to the
party. He served as county treasurer faithfully from 1870 to 1874,
and then resumed the loan business, adding to it the livery business,
going into partnership with N. Thomas. Since then, he had devoted
himself to both enterprises, becoming sole proprietor of the livery
stable. As a loan agent he was very successful, business reverses
came to him several years ago.

10

He was married on December 17, 1889, at Hartford, Conn., to Miss
Carrie Maude Hamilton, who has been a devoted wife. To them was
born one son, Leo Gutelius, on January 20, 1891.

The funeral services were held last Sunday afternoon (th 7th) at
the deceased's late residence. The attendance of friends from
Ashland and the surrounding communities was quite large. The services
were conducted by Rev. D. B. Duncan, of the Presbyterian church.

ANNA CAROLINE YEARICK

Anna Caroline Yearick was born February 19, 1829, at Raversburg, Center
County, Pa. (Known to her family as Aunt Callie, she never married.
She was a dressmaker by trade, and at one time, had a large shop in
Toledo where she employed fourteen girls. She lived the last years
of her life at the Widows Home in Toledo, passing away on February 1,
1915, at the age of 86. She is buried in Woodlawn Cemetery, Toledo.)

FREDERICK EMANUEL YEARICK

Frederick Emanuel Yearick was born September 26, 1830, at Brushvalley,
Center County, Pa.

SARAH CATHERINE YEARICK

Sarah Catherine Yearick was born February 9, 1832, at Brushvalley, Center County, Pa. She married twice. Her first husband was a man named
Switzer; the second was Albright.

REBECCA SUSSANNA YEARICK

Born September 3, 1834, in Wayne (now Ashland) County, Ohio, and died
July 19, 1851, in Ashland County.

(DR.) SAMUEL WILLIAM YEARICK

Born September 2, 1836, in Wayne (now Ashland) County, Ohio. (Died
1910, Cedar Rapids, Iowa.)

MARY ANN YEARICK

Born March 24, 1838, in Wayne (now Ashland) County, Ohio. She married John Lane. (Lived at Milford, Nebraska.)

JOHN AGUSTUS YEARICK

Was born April 14, 1840, in Ashland County, Ohio. (Lived at Iowa City, Iowa.)

JOSEPH PETER YEARICK

See Part II, page 1.

SIMON AMANDAS YEARICK

Was born November 22, 1845, in Ashland County, Ohio. (Lived at Woodward, Oklahoma.)

# # # # #

MR. & MRS. WILLIAM P. WARREN

Mr. and Mrs. William P. Warren were married December 20, 1836, in Washington County, New York, town of Hartford.

William Perkins Warren was born at Hartford on February 3, 1812, and died at the homestead near Sulphur Springs (Richards Station) April 8, 1870, of inflamation of the bowels. For many years he suffered from bronchial consumption and erysiphalis. The erysiplas was caused by wheat rust getting into his blood, and when it would heal up his cough was worse.

Mr. Warren was twice married. His first wife was Sally Bull. After the death of Sally, he married her sister, Laura Bull. Sally Bull was born on November 7, 1813, in Washington County, New York, and died April 7, 1852, at the homestead. Laura Bull was born on April 22, 1820, and died October 2, 1895 at the homestead.

To William Perkins Warren were born by his first wife, Zilpha (married to Thomas Carey) November 5, 1837; Oscar, November 15, 1839; Adelaide (married to J. P. Yearick) February 21, 1841; Marion (married to Orin Dority) January 26, 1848; and Sarah Mahala (married to Milo Warn) January 27, 1850. By his second wife, whom he married April 12, 1853, the following: Maurice, who died at the age of nine months, and Eugene, December 30, 1855.

Note: Following dates as near correct as practical.

ZILPHA WARREN

Was married to Thomas Carey November 5, 1859. They had eleven children, though only five grew up. Will was born about 1861 and died in the fall of 1898. Frank (date of birth not known) was killed in the wreck

of a building at Rochester, New York, while still a young man. Winnie
was born in 1865 or thereabouts, and Mary about 1869. Edith was born
in 1879.

OSCAR WARREN

Oscar Warren married Ella McIntyre in 1865 at Monroe, Michigan. To
them were born: Ora in 1866, Elmer in 1868, Orno in 1871, Edith in
1875, Ivan in 1878, and Mabel in 1885.

ADELAIDE WARREN.

See Part II.

MARION WARREN

Marion (f.) Warren married Orin Dority February 28, 1872. (He died
May 6, 1905.) To them were born: Anna Laura in 1874, Earl in 1876,
Grace in 1877, and Ross in 1882. A first born died in infancy.

SARAH MAHALA WARREN

Married Milo Warn (sic) October 6, 1870. (He died July 3, 1903.) To
them were born Burton in 1872, and Harry Howard in 1876.

EUGENE WARREN

Married Mina Clark February 28, 1879. To them were born: Minnie in
1880, Effie in 1885, and Carlton in 1895.

#####

PART V

Ancestors of

MRS. ANNA CATHERINE YEARICK, NEE GUTELIUS

Adam Frederick Gutelius, the first of the name of which there is any
record, is supposed to have been a Frenchman, and was educated for
an army surgeon by the government under which he lived.

His son, John Peter Gutelius, intermarried with Anne Maria Deitzler,
came to this country at an early, but unknown date, and in Lancaster
County, Pa., December 26, 1766, Frederick Gutelius was born to them.
In the course of time he became a blacksmith. Later he studied surveying. He married Catherine Bistel on the 31st day of August, 1790.
They moved to Mifflinburg, Pa., about the year 1800, using one two-
horse team for transporting their goods, while the family followed on
foot.

He served as esquire (justice of the peace) many years and did much
surveying and conveying, as the records show. He died on the 30th of
May, 1839. His wife died on the 11th of May, 1838. Both are buried
in the east end of the so-called Old Graveyard at Mifflinburg.

They had eleven sons and four daughters. Sarah married Samuel Grove.
Elizabeth married Jacob Dietrich. Anna Catherine married Peter
Yearick. Anne Maria died in infancy. William, the oldest son, died
in infancy. William, the second son, was born in 1794; died in 1857,
and never moved out of the old homestead. Samuel Gutelius was born
in 1795, and died in Likens Valley, Pa., about 1879. He was a prominent Reformed minister. He had six children.

John Frederick Gutelius was born in 1797; lived in Mifflinburg, Pa., all his life; was a dyer and weaver; raised twelve children, of whom Thomas, William, John, Jacob, Samuel, Charles, Caroline, Catherine and Mary Lydia were still living in 1889. Their mother was a daughter of Jacob Crotzer, and a sister to William Crotzer.

John Peter was born in 1798, and died about 1877. He had two children.

David was born in 1802, and died in Ohio in 1879. He had four children.

Israel was born in 1803, and died in Selinsgrove, Pa., about 1860. He had children, how many not known.

Henry was born in 1806, died in York County, Pa., in 1876. He had six children.

Andrew was born in 1808, was married to Lydia Fisher, and had three children: Mrs. John Romig and Mrs. Amanda Romig of Mifflinburg, and Rev. Fisher Gutelius of Moscow, New York.

George was born in 1812, was married to Catherine Alsbach; had eight children; lived in Mifflinburg all his life; was a cabinetmaker and foundryman; died in 1889.

Joseph was born in 1815; was married to Elizabeth Garrett. They had five children, of whom Albert, Elliot and Sarah Oliva of Mifflinburg, Pa., were the only survivors in 1889. He was killed in 1866 by a part of a tree falling on his head in the woods south of Mifflinburg.

While much of the history of this remarkable family must be omitted, it is due to say that it is noted for its patriotism and piety from its earliest existence.

The following article regarding Mrs. Sarah Gutelius Grove appeared in a Mifflinburg newspaper shortly after her demise.

This aged lady, who lived with her daughter, Mrs. Samuel Hoffman, on Market street, near the Reformed church, entered peacefully into her last rest on Saturday evening, April 29, 1893, at six o'clock. She was born in Mifflinburg January 4, 1811. Her age at death, therefor, was eighty-two years, three months and twenty-six days.

She was a widow twenty years, her husband, Samuel Grove, having died in 1873. She leaves three children: Mrs. Anna M. Lucas of Fremont, Ohio; Mrs. S. C. Hoffman and Mr. S. G. Grove of Mifflinburg. Mrs. Grove came from an honorable ancestry. Her grand-father Gutelius was one of those members of the Reformed chuch of France, who was driven out of his native land by intolerable persecution on account of his religion. This fact, perhaps, accounts in part, for the strong Christian character of Mrs. Grove herself. She was a most devout member of the Reformed church all her lifetime. Without bigotry, without parading her own piety and with great charity for all Christians, her own church was very dear to her. In her youth she was one of the first Sunday School scholars in the Old Elias church. Afterwards she became a teacher, until age and infirmity prevented her from meeting her class. Because of her long service in the Sunday School she became a teacher of teachers. Her familiarity with the scriptures is well known among all her friends. To the end of her long life she seemed to live in the presence of the spiritual world. And when the end came it was calm and peaceful as if she were only falling asleep.

In the death of Mrs. Grove another link in the chain that binds the present to the past generation is severed. From the church militant to the church triumphant the change for which she longed came at last. Her memory is blessed.

Ancestors of

MR. AND MRS. WILLIAM P. WARREN

The parents of William Perkins Warren were William Warren, a distant
relative of General Warren of Bunker Hill fame, and Mahala Warren, nee
Perkins.

The mother of Sally Warren, nee Bull, was Mary Foster. Mary and a
sister, Betsy Corbit, came to this country from the British Isles.
(Faint recollections favor Ireland.) Mr. and Mrs. Bull had children:
Minerva, Sally, Sally (sic) - the second of that name, Caroline,
Betsy, Mary, Lydia Ann, Saphrona, William, Nathaniel, John and another
whose name is unknown, but might have been Laura.

The children of William Warren and Mahala Perkins Warren are as follows:
Zilpha, whose first husband was Stephen Jackson. Her second husband
was a widower, Chancelor Ensign, who for his first wife married
Zilpha's sister Sarah. The offspring of Chancelor Ensign by his
first wife were: Elizabeth, Andrew, Mahala (who married Worthy Meade),
and Warren. Elizabeth and Andrew Ensign were schoolmates of Mary J.
Holmes, the noted authoress.

Alfred had daughters three. Mary married a Whitmore, Eliza, a Toby,
and Frances, a Sweet. Mr. and Mrs. Sweet are living on the old
Warren homestead (1899) in Washington County, New York, town of Hartford.

Betsy was also twice married. Her first husband was a man named Curtis.
For a second she took David Talford, the father-in-law of her daughter
Mariette, who had married Thomas Talford. Another daughter by Curtis,
Sarah Jane married John Brown (not the one famous in history and song).
John and Sarah Brown had five children: Mary, Susie, Andrew, Corie,
and another.

Clarisa married a man named Spring. They had children: William, July
Ann, Clarisy, Mary, Edwin, and David.

17